T 7153

D0689710

WITHDRAWN

DATE DUE

JUN 2001	APR 2 1 2015		
JUL 1 1 2001	SEP 1 0 2015		
NOV 2 1 2001	DEC 0 1 2016		
APR. 0 3 2002			
DEC. 29 2004			
SEP. 0 3 2005			
MAR. 1 1 2007			
DEC. 1 5 2007			
JUL 0 1 2008			
MAR 0 5 2011			
MAR 1 8 2015			

this
·little·barron's·
book belongs to

....

....

For Laura

AE

First edition for the United States and Canada published 1999 by
Barron's Educational Series, Inc.

Copyright text © Sally Grindley 1999
Copyright illustrations © Andy Ellis 1999

First published in Great Britain by Orchard Books in 1999.

All inquiries should be addressed to:
Barron's Educational Series, Inc.
250 Wireless Boulevard, Hauppauge, New York 11788
http://www.barronseduc.com

Library of Congress Catalog Card No.: 98-74973
International Standard Book No. 0-7641-0870-0

Printed in Italy

20174

this
·little·barron's·
book belongs to

....

....

For Laura

AE

First edition for the United States and Canada published 1999 by
Barron's Educational Series, Inc.

Copyright text © Sally Grindley 1999
Copyright illustrations © Andy Ellis 1999

First published in Great Britain by Orchard Books in 1999.

All inquiries should be addressed to:
Barron's Educational Series, Inc.
250 Wireless Boulevard, Hauppauge, New York 11788
http://www.barronseduc.com

Library of Congress Catalog Card No.: 98-74973
International Standard Book No. 0-7641-0870-0

Printed in Italy

20174

Elephant Small
Goes to a Party

Sally Grindley • Andy Ellis

• little • barron's •

Elephant Small was very excited because he had been invited to Jolly Dog's birthday party.

"Time to get ready," said Elephant Mom.
"WHOOPEE!" said Elephant Small.

Elephant Mom began to wrap up Jolly Dog's present.
"Can I do it?" asked Elephant Small.

"Put your trunk there," said Elephant Mom. "OUCH!" cried Elephant Small. "You stuck me as well."

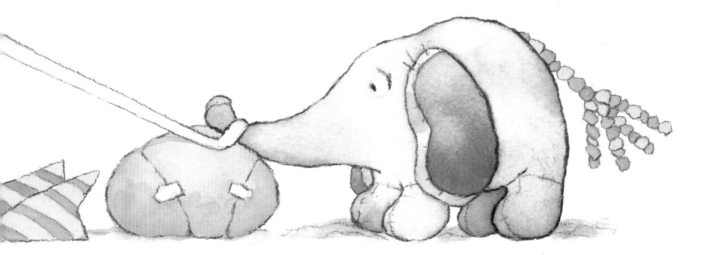

Elephant Mom took Elephant Small
over to the party. Jolly Dog bounced up
to greet them.

"Give Jolly Dog his present," said
Elephant Mom.
"Can't I keep it?" said Elephant Small.
"It's not your birthday," said
Elephant Mom.

"Aren't you staying with me?" asked
Elephant Small.
"No," said Elephant Mom, "but all your
friends are here."

"I'll be scared without you," whispered Elephant Small.
"You'll have fun," said Elephant Mom, "and I'll be back soon."

"Don't be shy," said Jolly Dog. "Come and have a fizzy drink."
Elephant Small sucked with his trunk.
SLURP!

But the bubbles made him sneeze
– ACHOO! – and he blew
Plastic Penguin's hat off.

"Time for musical chairs," said Jolly Dog.

Elephant Small watched, then he joined in. Then he got so excited, he missed the chair and sat on Loppy Rabbit.

"Now it's time for my birthday cake," said Jolly Dog.

Elephant Small was so excited, he waved his trunk — SPLAT! — and splashed cream all over Clockwork Mouse.

"Did you miss me?" said Elephant Mom
when she came to collect him.

Elephant Small was so excited, he didn't
know what to tell her about first.
"We had games and food and cake and . . .
and . . . when can I have a party, Mommy?"